D1562855

The
Other Side
of Fear

Maria Anderson

Cover design, illustration, and book design
by Amanda Hughes

Published by The Wrighting on the Walls, LLC

For those who fear the darkness and push through to the
other side.

Michelle,

There's always
a rainbow on the
other side of
fear.

Maria
-2021-

Also by Maria Anderson

Learning to Love Yourself:
A 10-Day Commitment to You

CHAPTER 1

I once read that children who grow up with alcoholic parents are four times more likely to become alcoholics themselves.

I'm Renee and I am not an alcoholic. I'm a successful marketing director for a large firm and I have everything together. At least that's what it looks like from the outside. Considering my mother was an alcoholic and my father was a rolling stone, I've done pretty well for myself. I'm married to a handsome, successful and loyal man, we have two amazing children who we truly adore, and I am happy.

I may be happy, but today I'm sitting in a pitch meeting bored out of my mind. *Do they really think this is a good marketing plan?* Knowing this idea will never work I sit back, smile and daydream. The cold chairs of the conference room take me back to a place I haven't thought about in years.

***

Uggghhh! The cold hard plastic crunches as my mother lays me on the couch at the blue house across the street. I don't understand why this lady's whole couch is wrapped in plastic. Does it not make her butt cold? I'm glad I only have to lay here for a little while before we head off to school.

I remember walks to school as clear in my head as if they occurred yesterday. But they didn't. That was well over 35 years ago. Little did I know, I was going to spend a lot of time on that couch in the mornings before school and less time with my mother.

***

The clock in the conference room suddenly sounds so loud as it brings me back into reality, and it is almost time for me to pick up my little minions, Alex and London. Lord Jesus, I love them but sometimes I wonder will they ever stop talking and where do they get all of their energy?!

London is my sweet angel who loves science more than Albert Einstein himself. She has blown up, spilled and "created" more concoctions than I can count on one hand. As a sixth grader, she is a rising star in her school, compared only to her older brother Alex, my super friendly son. That boy would make friends with the squirrel outside if he thought it was lonely. He has his daddy's smile; it gets him out of all the trouble he *should* get into. Alex and London are definitely my pride and joy. James and I have worked very hard to provide more for them than we had as children. They have no idea how good they have it and we're okay with that.

"Mommy, today in science Ms. Bailey was teaching about energy and I thought of a really good plan for the rollercoaster I want to build," London says as soon as she gets into the car.

"Mommy, we're selling chocolates so we can go to Six Flags for our class trip. Can you take them to work?" Alex says as he tries to overtalk his sister.

I interrupt the children's ongoing conversation, "Can we start over again? Hello, children."

"Hi Mommy," they say in unison, taking a quick breath as they continue to fight over who will tell me all about their day first.

We begin our daily drive home through Atlanta traffic; God, I hate this traffic. Spaghetti Junction. 20 West. Georgia 400. All of them have way too many people packed onto them rushing to get somewhere, anywhere and everywhere at the same time.

Alex and London continue talking in the back seat, "Mommy, Alex used his lunch money on desserts again today," London gladly informs me.

"Snitch," Alex not-so-quietly says under his breath.

I absentmindedly start to run through the list of tasks that I need to accomplish tonight when we get home: dinner, homework, school clothes for tomorrow, prayers and bedtime for the kids. After all of that, it's Renee time, which consists of a long, hot shower and preparation for my honey to come home. James has been away on a business trip. I don't know why, but this has been the longest four days ever. I can't wait until he gets home, and I get to feel his lips again.

"MOMMY! Are you listening?" Alex yells from the back seat.

"I'm sorry Alex, honey. What did you say?" I reply.

"Mr. Charles gave us a Social Studies assignment to complete. A family tree. It's due next week. I know most of Daddy's family, but I don't know what to put for your side."

"Hmmm, neither do I, Alex. We'll figure it out together."

When the kids were younger and I introduced them to pictures of my relatives, I started calling my mother "Ms. Virginia." I mean, she didn't really take care of me, so "Mom" sounded like a title that didn't fit who she was to me. She was an incubator who gave me life and who loved me as much as she was capable despite not being able to love herself.

The kids knew that I was raised by my grandma, who passed away the year before Alex was born. Alex and London both call her "GG-ma." It was short for great-grandmother and much easier to teach them as toddlers. Though they have never met her, GG-ma adorns the walls of our home and I often share stories of growing up with her. GG-ma saved me. She deserved a title.

***

As the hot water trickles over my hair, I can't help but think of Alex's assignment. How will I explain to my son that my family tree is more like a forest, a scary, dark forest filled with tall trees with thorns, lots of boulders and creatures that can hurt you if you let them?

While the hot shower washes over my body, my mind escapes to a time many years in the past, inside the forest. The scary dark forest that holds memories that I've worked really hard to forget.

***

As we sit in the uncomfortable chairs at the halfway house, my mother proudly tells all of the residents that I am her baby. But the truth was, I haven't been a baby in years. I've been cooking breakfast, lunch and dinner for myself for at least six years now. When my mother disappeared on a drinking binge, I would check the neighborhood liquor stores, park benches and normal hiding spots for "homeless" people. My mother wasn't homeless, but she was hopeless, and I was ready to escape this halfway house, my mother and the entire experience.

She's holding another 30-day chip, smiling from ear to ear, proud of her accomplishment. She'll gift it to me "so that I know she's serious this time." The chip is always accompanied with an apology for the impact of her drinking.

I'll add it to the collection of other 30-day chips that I have received through the years. I also have a few 60-day chips and one rare 90-day chip.

My mother didn't make it to many meetings after 90 days because in her own words, "I don't need those meetings anymore. The coffee is horrible. And I can bake a cake far better than that crap they serve there."

It may sound a little bitter, but I feel like this journey of having an alcoholic mother has led me down roads I've had to travel repeatedly. And even though she's been there in some form or another, my mother has always left me feeling alone. The chips, 90-day or 9,000 days are simply a reminder of the roads I've had to travel often and alone.

Even when we had a warm roof over our head, being a child taking care of an adult was always an adventure. This often involved me cleaning up her spilled drink when she passed out in the bed. My dinners were usually prepared in the Easy Bake Oven and occasionally in the broiler. The ultra-thick welfare cheese melted better in the broiler than on the stove. I perfected toast with cheese to the point where the bread was nice and crispy, and the cheese was melted just right with only a few small brown spots.

There were constant deliveries, often with CODs. Cash on Delivery, or CODs were offered by the company that allowed you to order something and pay for it when it was delivered. More often than not we couldn't afford to pay for the stuff my mother would order. That didn't prevent her from ordering it, though. My mother loved porcelain dolls. The kind that stood on stands, with perfect little curls, perfect dresses and perfect shoes. They were way too perfect for our dysfunctional house.

Thank goodness I have my grandma around to make sure I have basic necessities. Grandma isn't my mother's mom or even my father's mom, she's the babysitter. But she takes care of me as if I was her own. She always has, ever since the first day my mother laid me on her plastic couch.

***

"Hey Babe."

The alluring sound of my man at the bathroom door snaps me back into the present. James is six-feet, two inches of tall, dark sexiness. His large physique is deceitful to people who do not know him. But my king is a gentle giant who has protected me in more ways than one since the first night that we met. James is one of the most attractive men I know. Even though it's taken me a while to believe it myself, he is also the most loyal man I know. He works hard to provide for his family. He's thoughtful, always sending me gifts when he's been away. And he still turns me on in all the ways that he did when we first met. I think

I'll stay in the shower a little longer if James will come join me.

***

CHAPTER 2

I've dropped the kids off at school and headed in to work, but first I'm going to swing past the new Starbucks on Piedmont. We just placed a huge building-length marketing campaign close by and I love to see the vision and planning of my work come into fruition. Venti Soy Chai with two pumps of sugar free vanilla, no water and no foam. As always, my drink is perfect, and the ad looks amazing! I proudly pat myself on the back and give a head nod at the reflection in the rearview mirror. *You are a badass, Renee*, I tell myself as I drive towards work.

My workday is filled with designing new ad campaigns, client meetings and distractions. Before I know it, the day is over, and I'm headed to my second job—H.M.I.C.—Head Mommy in Charge.

I'm in the mood for a real meal tonight: beef ribs, macaroni and cheese, green beans and, of course, cornbread. Shortly after moving to Atlanta, I learned that every good Southern meal must be accompanied by homemade cornbread. I am from Boston, so homemade cornbread is a stretch, but by the time I finish adding special ingredients to the Jiffy mix, you would think it was homemade cornbread.

As I finish preparing tonight's dinner, I hear the kids updating their daddy on everything that he missed out on while he was away. James is so good with them. He listens so attentively, and they have the longest conversations.

I innocently eavesdrop on their conversation from the kitchen. Alex and London are intent on sharing every detail of the past four days; they are tripping over themselves to talk to James. He laughs at all the right places. Asks the right questions. Without knowing, he reinforces life lessons I've shared with the kids throughout the week about being kind, sharing with others and just being a good person. We're on the same page even when he's been away. I stop eavesdropping long enough to fix the plates and call everyone to the table for dinner.

As I walk into the dining room with full plates, a smile on my face and in my heart, Alex tells me, "Mommy, daddy's next work trip is to Boston. Can we go with him? Then you can show us where you grew up and we can finally finish my family tree."

That isn't exactly the "oh" and "ah" I was hoping for as I walked the plates to the table.

I think to myself, *I totally thought we nipped this family tree thing in the bud: me, my mother, my father and Grandma, Grandad and Uncle Rob— that's it; that's all I got for you, kid.* I've done a lot of work to keep the secrets of the dark forest *in* the forest. Why will my child not leave this alone? I've forgotten about the monsters inside the forest and I don't plan on visiting them anytime soon.

I refocus my attention on dinner and say, "Alex, we can discuss that later." I set the plates at each table setting and grab one of Alex and London's hands. I kiss the back of my beautiful children's hands and look at James. "Will you say grace, please?"

During dinner, Alex and London continue the Spanish Inquisition regarding James' business trip to Boston. London is focused on the numerous museums that she wants to visit. Alex is focused on going to a Celtics game and hoping to meet one of the players. With each bite of food they take, they come up with another question for the trip. By the end of dinner, they have planned the entire trip, including sightseeing and visiting Ms. Virginia.

Just the idea of returning back to the city that created me gives me such angst and instantly puts me in a bad mood.

Each time the kids ask me a question about Ms. Virginia, my mouth just so happens to be full of food. I am not getting sucked into the rabbit hole with the children tonight. I answer the kids' questions about Boston and what our special trip will be like while quickly swallowing my food, little chewing involved. After seconds are served and the food disappears, I clear the table and begin to clean up the kitchen while the kids get ready for bed and James works on his computer. Several minutes pass until we are summoned to the kids' rooms for bedtime routines. We say prayers together as a family, topping off the night with kisses on the forehead for each child. Hand in hand, James and I walk together to wind down and get ready for bed.

***

As James gets into the shower, I sit at the vanity and comb through my hair, thinking. Both children had a ton of questions about Mrs. Virginia and

Boston questions that I didn't want to answer and still don't.

James can always tell when there is something on my mind. I can feel him watching me through the shower doors while he is showering. I hear him ask loudly over my thoughts, "Babe, there's a lot the kids don't know about you." He knows how I feel about my past, so I am not sure why he is engaging in this conversation. I smile at him in the shower, turning to walk into the bedroom. Climbing into bed, I grab my newest novel, *The Scars We Chose*, by one of my favorite authors, A. Lee Hughes. This book is the escape I need from that ridiculous conversation.

I hear the shower turn off and James soon joins me in the bedroom.

"I know there is a lot of hurt in your past, Renee. But wouldn't it be nice for you to show the kids a little of who you are?"

Nice? I think to myself. *More like torture!*

"I'm going to fix a drink. Would you like something?" I ask him but I walk out of the room before he can answer. I need a moment to think.

Nice. Humph. *As if.*

Talking about the past is annoying, draining and has no purpose.

James didn't have an easy childhood either. His father wasn't around so his mother and her family were his main support system. He understands my drive and determination because he always wanted more than what he had growing up as well. But he doesn't truly understand how unstable my childhood was. It's a wonder I made it through my teenage years without multiple kids or multiple clinic visits like so many other girls from my neighborhood. I don't know if James understands how deep the hurt goes.

Before I met him, I spent a lot of time running from my past—moving from state to state, attempting to create a better future and crying into my pillow at night. James was the stability that I had been seeking. He is a great, loyal man, unlike most of the men I knew. Including the one who contributed to half my DNA.

My father, on the other hand, had a lot of female "friends" through the years. How was I supposed to explain that to James and the kids? Christy. Amanda. Tina. Debra.

While I walk to the kitchen for that drink, my mind wanders back to Debra, specifically.

***

I walk up the steps to ring the doorbell of the tan-colored apartment door, double-checking the address my father gave me over the phone a few days ago. He answers the door, smiling, and gestures for me to come in. "This is Debra, my new girlfriend." That's how my dad introduced me to his latest flavor of the week. I don't plan on remembering her name. They don't last long, and he'll disappear soon anyway. These visits are such a waste of time. But I promised Grandma that I would try to have a relationship with this man.

"What's new, Pumpkin?" my father asks. The question sounds like a desperate attempt at making small talk.

And he's the only person who calls me "Pumpkin," which is super annoying.

"My mother was passed out again last night, but don't worry, I made sure she was okay," I respond sarcastically to my absent philandering father.

Sure, I am behaving like a snotty teenager but rightfully so! My father's girlfriends come and go like a revolving door. Debra is going to learn today that when it comes to my father what glitters isn't always gold. In fact, it's usually just a shiny pile of poop. There are so many other places I would rather be right now. But I will do what's right, even if none of the adults who created me will.

"Debra introduced me to this fruit," my father said, the small talk killing me. "It's called 'kiwi.' Try it. You might like it."

I look at the slimy green fruit with black seeds in it. I give an "are you serious" look with my eyes, scrunching up my lips and nose as I look from the fruit to my father's face. "Umm, yeah, no. But thanks," I decline.

Two more awkward hours of getting to know Debra is going to suck! I'm sure she thinks I am a typical teenager—she has no idea. Showing my ass is almost as much fun as watching her uneasy attempts at stumbling through a conversation with me.

I jump up quickly when the clock strikes six. Like one of those turkey timer button things, I pop from the sofa, say my goodbyes and fly out the door for the bus stop.

Mission accomplished. I spent time with my father.

***

"Babe," James interrupts my thoughts and I look up from the glass that I've been holding, the ice having nearly melted. "You've been down here for an hour. Are you okay?"

I set the glass on the counter and swipe at my wet face. I hadn't even known I was crying. "Yeah, babe," I sigh. "Let's go to bed."

***

"Now boarding flight 1908 to Boston," the gate attendant announces with her Southern accent strong over the static-filled speakers. She looks around at the anxious and ready-to-board guests who have moved closer and closer to her podium. With a slight attitude, she announces, "We'll start with our Business Class customers first. Please have your boarding pass in your hand and prepare all carry-on items."

How the hell did I end up at the airport, boarding a plane and headed to Boston? Oh, that's right, James' work trip and Alex's never-ending questions. This is so typical of my family. Always the supportive mother and loving wife, I'll do whatever needs to be done to make the family happy. So, a few days in Boston it is—its' not like I don't have work of my own to do. And now London has jumped onto the Boston bandwagon and created a list of museums she wants to visit during the trip. First stop, Museum of Science, of course.

I think my family is secretly trying to take me out. I am going to need some liquid courage to keep it together on this flight.

Not long after we're settled in the seats on the plane, the flight attendant starts to make her rounds and take drink orders. That is one of the bonus aspects of being in Business Class. Roomier seats. Ample carry-on space. Plenty of leg room, which is really important for James. And drinks before the flight exits onto the runway.

"I'll take a vodka and seltzer with a lime. Heavy on the vodka, light on the seltzer, please," I say to the flight attendant.

James orders his normal Crown and Coke. The kids order sodas rather loudly as they yell over whatever movie they are watching on their MacBooks.

The flight attendant responds quickly, and I thank her as I order a second drink—just in case she gets too busy later.

The plane continues the boarding process, filling rather rapidly. The flight attendants begin the requisite flight safety instructions and prepare for liftoff.

As the airplane barrels down the runway, I close my eyes and my mind wanders.

How familiar will Boston be? It's been so many years since I was there—it feels like a different lifetime. Will I remember the streets that I travelled so frequently as a kid? Or will I be like the tourists who walk the streets every day?

I take another sip of my drink, place my AirPods in my ears, hit Play on Beyonce's latest album, pull out my book and escape into another reality.

***

CHAPTER 3

Well, it still sounds the same—horns blaring, music blasting, car brakes screeching to unexpected halts, people yelling on the corner. I haven't been to Boston in 15 years. Things look different yet very much the same. Such a juxtaposition.

We've come a few days before James' meetings start so that we can spend some time exploring the city together as a family. London has already mapped out the Museum of Science; she wants to visit the newest exhibit on the human body, and, of course, the triceratops exhibit. According to London's planning, the Children's Museum is "too childish" for her. She would much rather visit the Peabody Museum of Archeology and Ethnology.

Alex's trip requests do not include museum visits. He wants to go to a Celtics game and get Jayson Tatum's autograph. Alex started watching basketball with his daddy several years ago. His daddy, an avid Kobe fan, loves the game and was so excited to share his love with Alex. However, Alex was only focused on the sneakers at first. Tatum always wears the newest and brightest shoes on the court; therefore, he became Alex's favorite player. In addition to going to the game, Alex wants to check out a few sneaker stores to see if they have different "kicks" than the ones in Atlanta. Oh, and of course he wants to visit Ms. Virginia, because that was the whole reason that we came to Boston.

I am just hoping for a nice 60-minute Swedish massage at the hotel, some quality Chinese food, fresh seafood and leaving the past in the past. Sounds easy enough.

We turn towards the Williams Tunnel and I instantly remember that the traffic here sucks almost as much as it does in Atlanta. More car horns. People leaning out of car windows swearing at the car who just cut them off. Buses everywhere. Yup, Boston is exactly the same.

***

I finished college, drove home to spend some quality time with Grandma, and then hit the road. I had enough of the snow, cold weather and dark forests. Grandma understood and she supported my move. I headed to Florida, the Happiest Place on Earth—what better place to find happiness? Florida was everything that Boston wasn't: slower pace, longer days full of sunshine and beaches where you could actually get into the water.

However, after six months of the beach every day, no real job lined up, and no newfound happiness, I decided to pack it up and head North, just a little bit, to Atlanta.

Atlanta was a great mixture of Boston and Florida. It was sunny, warm and fast-paced. Traffic was a little insane but nothing I wasn't used to from home. I felt like the city welcomed me with open arms. It didn't hurt that my high school best friend Nicole lived there. We hit the Atlanta party scene and left no rock unturned. When I wasn't going on interviews for a marketing job, I was serving tables at the local Applebee's Restaurant.

What do they say? "Time flies when you're having fun"? Well, I was having an amazing time in Atlanta. It was easy to make the city my new home. It had everything that I needed: nightlife, a good job, a new apartment and a dependable friend. I talked to Grandma every other day during the week and after church every Sunday. Which was perfect because Nicole and I usually got in way too late from the club on Saturday night.

I hustled and developed a good life for myself in Atlanta, returning to Boston briefly only to lay Grandma to rest. Once Grandma passed, I didn't have a reason to go back to Boston. In my past, however, the dark forests were around every corner and the memories still haunted me.

My new life in Atlanta was full of laughter and good times at Club 112, a popular Atlanta nightspot where I also met James. I'll never forget that moment: a crisp New Year's Eve night with my best friend by my side and champagne in-hand. It was the night when I finally found the happiness I'd sought for so long in Boston and Florida.

***

When I was growing up, the Boston Commons was a magical place where only the tourists visit. Us real Bostonians didn't have neither time nor interest in riding a plastic, swan-shaped boat around a murky pond. So often I'd walked past that park headed towards Downtown Crossing. Never make eye contact with the homeless people—that was the rule. Unless it's your mother. And, in that case, you walked a little faster.

As I look across the street from our tenth-floor suite, I can visualize my mother in that park. Days when I found her there were a struggle; those were her rock-bottom moments. There were many but not always the Boston Commons; there were other parks she would elect to sleep in as well.

I didn't share my family struggle with many of my friends; it was *my* struggle, not theirs. And since there was nothing they could do to help, why bother telling them? Besides, my life was just perfect living with Grandma.

Yeah, my mother kind of stopped paying the rent. When the police came to evict us, she grabbed her porcelain dolls. I grabbed my Easy Bake oven. I asked the officer to take me to my grandma's house. My mother, well she was going to be homeless, but I was going to a warm home.

If Grandma was surprised to see me at her doorstep with the police, she sure didn't show it. She simply told me to head to the shower and leave the "toy" in the bedroom. As I nestled into the bed, Grandma came up to say prayers with me.

"Renee, your mother loves you," I remember Grandma saying to me after prayers.

"I know," I replied.

"You can stay here as long as you need to. You're our family and this will always be your room," she said while gently kissing me on my forehead. She ducked to avoid the slanted wall and headed downstairs.

I laid in the bed thinking to myself, *Calling this a room might be a bit of a stretch.* I was in the attic. Grandma's son, Rob, was in the room across the hall. When I first arrived to Grandma's house, he was a pain in my ass. He was the annoying big brother that I never wanted. Teasing and picking on me constantly. What kids nowadays would call "bullying." Oh, Grandma would fuss at him, "Rob, leave that girl alone before I kick your balls up and down the street!"

I would chuckle every time she said this; as unrealistic as it was is, it was still funny as hell. Rob and I truly became like brother and sister through the years. I ended up staying with Grandma until I graduated from high school. While I was there, I had a bed, a home and a family.

***

"Mommy, when you grew up here, did you ever see the ducklings from the book?" London asks.

"No, London. I didn't spend much time down in the Commons as a kid. But we can definitely go look for them tomorrow, my dear," I reply, already mentally exhausted from this trip.

Copley Plaza! Oh, the memories! The boys I

kissed at that train station, the window shopping my friends and I did on a weekly basis. We never bought anything except candy; that was all we could afford. We always stopped at the candy shop and picked our favorite color gummies out of the bin. Shoot, if I was paying for it, I was going to get what I wanted.

Today, we're on a boat-slash-car that's shaped like a duck taking a tour of the city. I have learned so much information that I never knew growing up here.

"How did you not learn this stuff, hon?" James asks, perplexed.

Well, babe, I was busy looking for my wandering mother and maintaining good grades in school so I could escape this place, I say rather loudly in my head. But I give him a much nicer response, "I don't know, dear. I guess it just never interested me."

As the plastic boat travels from land to sea, I share stories from my childhood with my family: hanging with my friends, walking from train station to train station just to avoid the higher fare. I share stories of shopping at Filene's Basement. The concept of shopping at a store in a basement is so foreign to my children; they can't understand why I would have wanted to shop there.

Because I was poor, dear children, because I

was poor.

Again, I choose a more appropriate response, "Because it was the cool thing to do."

While James and the kids point out all of the places I used to visit when I lived here, I remember teenager Renee who wore bamboo earrings, at least two pairs, had a pager hanging from her pocket and a gold chain around her neck.

***

"Miss, Miss come to see me; I can beat their price," A booth merchant calls out, trying to steal us from the current booth.

"Why do you need a Tweety Bird necklace again?" my father asks me.

"You asked what I wanted for my birthday. That's it," I reply with just a little snark.

Why is my father standing in the Jewelry Exchange trying to rationalize with me? This is our "weekly date," as my grandma calls it. We usually only do dinner, but my birthday is in a few days and my disappearing father has no idea what to get me.

So, here we are in the Jewelry Exchange, a building filled with gold, silver, something resembling diamonds and anything else you could think of, including the newest teenage craze:

pagers.

A pager was this little electronic device that could receive messages and signals. My friends and I would page each other 9-1-1 when we needed a callback so we could gossip about something stupid a boy said or did.

This is our second date since Grandma had to put my father in his place. I was sent to my room while they talked, but I heard Grandma say, "I need one of you to get your head out of your ass and get to know your kid."

I chuckled. At four feet, five inches, with heels on, Grandma was fierce.

***

CHAPTER 4

I barely hear London say, "Daddy, mommy is doing that weird smile thing again." I snap back to reality, roll my eyes and hug my sweet baby girl. She is so much like me, it's a shame. Speaks her mind and confident in everything that comes out of her mouth. I am not looking forward to her teenage years.

James was right, these moments with the kids are priceless. Boston may look and sound the same, but I am not the same person who left here 15 years ago. James is not my father, he is consistently good, loyal and loving. London is daddy's little girl; she has him wrapped around her finger—as it should be. I love every moment of it. As this plastic boat continues to travel, I think to myself, *Maybe this will be a good trip home after all.*

***

"Mommy, will we see Ms. Virginia while we're here?" Alex has asked me this question one way or another since he learned about his daddy's business trip to Boston. This child is determined to learn about the woman who carried me in her stomach for nine months.

Well, at least I think it was nine months; I'm not really sure about my early childhood. There are no baby books like the ones that I incessantly completed for both of my children. There's no secret email where my mother wrote notes for me throughout my childhood. And even though email wasn't a thing around the time when I was born, I still firmly believe that were it an option, this type of gesture never would have happened for me. My mother just wasn't that type of mother. She wasn't capable of being that type of mother.

To be honest, even if I were looking for her, I wouldn't even know where to start. When I left for college, my communication was limited. My mother was always moving from place to place, shelter to shelter, rooming house to rooming house. I didn't talk to her often. Even if I were able to contact her whenever I wanted, I can honestly say I don't know if I would have. I was angry. I was tired of being disappointed. I wanted a mother who could love, support and guide me. Virginia couldn't do any of that. She was still giving me 30-day chips whenever she stumbled.

If shelter residents wanted assistance in finding an apartment, they had to guarantee that they were alcohol and drug-free. My mother would hit rock bottom, end up at the shelter and get clean again. With each milestone of being alcohol-free, she received a new chip to celebrate her sobriety. The chips are meant to be a visual reminder to the alcoholic that someone is there to understand and support them. My mother went through these steps quite a few times and by the time I went to college, I had more than my share of chips. By that time, I was sick of the damn chips.

I went to college and tried to put the past behind me. That meant that I disconnected myself as much as possible from my life in Boston. I spoke to Grandma regularly, though. Grandma saved me from a never-ending cycle and provided some stability. It wasn't perfect but I learned that no family was perfect, they were all just surviving.

***

I may not have called every week, but I also didn't

completely neglect my mother. When she was clean and found a place to stay, I visited. It was weird; she loved me, but it felt like she didn't know me. That was my mother's fault. She made the choice to keep drinking. She could have chosen her daughter over the alcohol at any point in time, but she didn't. In fact, she didn't choose any of her children over the alcohol. That's right, I have two brothers; they were raised in Alabama with their real grandmother. I know of them, but we don't have a relationship and I'm okay with that.

By my sophomore year in college, the alcohol had slowly eaten away at my mother's memory. It's such a confusing feeling to know someone loves you but they continuously disappoint you. I remember going to her apartment and checking for evidence of liquor, specifically Bacardi. Oh, she had a favorite: Bacardi and Sprite. No need for cups, she would just mix it right in the Sprite bottle. So classy. I couldn't drink Sprite for the longest time because it made me mad. It was as if somehow I blamed Sprite for taking my mother away from me. As an adult, that sounds silly as hell to admit. As a kid, it made perfect sense.

***

"How about this," I say to the kids, my memories of my mother fading. "While Daddy is in meetings today, I will show you some of the neighborhoods that I grew up in."

London and Alex's eyes grow large and the smiles slowly spread across their faces. They both look at me in apprehension, wondering if I am serious. I nod my head in reassurance and they both jump off the couch, smiling from ear to ear. Before long, they are at the hotel room door with phones in-hand, AirPods in their ears and sweaters, just in case. As for me, I put on jeans, a T-shirt, and a pair of Toms—I think I'm physically ready for this adventure.

***

Silver Slipper, a restaurant famous for some of the best breakfast sandwiches in town, is our first stop. The old neighborhood looks a little different but sounds exactly the same. Dudley Station, where the buses come and go to move passengers all around town. Nubian Notion, a staple African Store that sells everything from sour pickles to incense. Joe's Famous Steak Subs hands-down has the best bombers in the world!

These places are long-standing treasures that have been in this neighborhood long before I was born. These streets are the same ones Malcolm Little walked before he became Malcolm X.

I park the car in a lot that wasn't here 15 years ago. The kids and I take a walking tour of a neighborhood that I became very familiar with during middle and high school. I tell the kids stories of calling Grandma collect from payphones in Dudley Station.

"Do you mean a cell phone?" asks Alex, confused.

"And what's collect?" asks London, equally confused.

"No, this was before cell phones. There were these 'boxes' where you could put change in and call people. But if you didn't have money, you could ask the operator to call someone collect and the person you were calling would pay for it."

"That's so weird," Alex says. "So, GG-Ma would pay for you to call her?"

"Oh, heck no! But that's another story for another day. Let's just say your mommy got really good at saying things very quickly." I giggle at those memories. I wouldn't dare expect Grandma to pay for me to call her. I got really good at saying what I needed when the tone asked for me to only say my name.

"GrandmaI'matDudleyStationI'mokayLoveYou"

As the kids and I walk around Dudley Station, I point out the mural painted on the side of Silver Slipper proudly displaying Malcolm X, the trains that used to run above the station and old scenes of the neighborhood. We enjoy sour pickles from Nubian Notion as we stroll down what used to be my daily path to school. Both kids agree my high school looks different than the monstrous school they attend back home in Atlanta.

As we near the projects behind the high school, I grab my kids' hands. I don't dare walk back there—I don't have the clout now that I once had back then. We gingerly stroll up the hill to my old middle school. It is mind-blowing to see my children on the same swings that I played on decades before. The first Black church in Boston still sits proudly across the street, as do the old brick buildings where New Edition used to hang out.

As we walk and talk, the kids are like sponges, soaking up all of my stories. I have to admit, my memories of Dudley Station and of high school are good. They mark a time when life transitioned from crazy and uncertain to stable and complete. Before driving back to the hotel, we stop at Joe's and order four of the greasiest steak and cheese bombers the kids have ever seen. This is the only place that does steak and cheese bombers with grace. You sit on the stool and watch as your steak sizzles on the grill, the chef chopping the meat non-stop as it cooks, adding in onions and green peppers while steadily flipping the meat. Right before it's done, the chef tops off the meat with four slices of white American cheese, letting it melt slightly before stuffing it into the softest sub roll you've ever tasted. There's no way I could be this close and not expose my family to this deliciousness.

The drive back to the hotel is short. I somehow remember all of the backroads to get us back downtown, completely avoiding the highway. As we pass the neighborhood homeless shelter, Pine Street Inn, I instinctively search the crowd for my mother. But she is no longer at this shelter. I couldn't tell you where she is now.

***

Back at the hotel, James is watching an episode of *Chicago P.D.* as we enter the suite. Holding up the bag containing the bombers from Joe's, Alex proudly tells his dad that we picked up dinner. Looking at the grease-soaked bag, James asks, "Is there anything in there besides grease?"

During dinner, London and Alex excitedly tell their daddy about our adventure. I listen as the kids attempt to describe pay phones and all of the different buses leaving Dudley Station. Their retelling of our day creates a different image of the Dudley that I left so long ago.

The kids see the goodness in the history of the neighborhood. They are in awe at how a high school could be so "small." They describe the swings in the old neighborhood park, and we all laugh as they recall what happened when I tried to get on one. Both mention that I went to school in the same neighborhood as some "old school group named New Edition." Their perspective is so new and fresh, untainted.

***

CHAPTER 5

After describing the events of the previous day, it didn't take much convincing to get James to come along today. This time we venture into Mattapan, the neighborhood where I grew up, where life started for me, I guess. Itasca Street looks the same, in a sense, yet totally different. Although none of the neighbors who lived here back when I was a kid seem to be here now, the houses are all still the same.

As we pull in front of the light blue house, I instantly get chills. The large Christmas light bulbs that hung year-round on the roof are no longer there. The fence leading to the backyard is rusted and barely on the hinges. I wonder if the pussy willow tree is still in the back. It was right next to

Grandma's bedroom window. There was the huge oak tree in the backyard, too. It used to leak sap in the springtime. Oh, how I hated when the tree was "home base" during a good game of freeze tag. I somehow always managed to put my hand right in the sap. So annoying.

I look across the street and the pale-yellow house is there, but I don't remember it as much. That is the house where my mother and father attempted to build a family. Until reality hit, Sprite and Bacardi secrets were uncovered, and mistresses became the final breaking point. In that house, there are some stairs that lead upstairs, but I only know this from the few pictures that I've seen. My mind has done a great job of blocking out most of the memories in this house. I guess it's my body's way of protecting me. I'm sure the forest of my childhood would be even darker if I remembered all of the trauma from the early days. I remember my mother sitting in the backyard cleaning fish that my dad had just brought back from a fishing trip. Scales flying everywhere. I enjoyed eating the fish but watching it being cleaned was not my idea of fun.

The walk across the street to Grandma's house seems so short now. I swear it felt like forever as my mother used to carry me from our house to Grandma's in the wee hours of the morning and then lay me on the freezing cold plastic couch. That's how my parents met the woman who would become my grandma. She was the neighborhood "safe" house. My parents both had decent careers but had to leave for work very early. So of course, the older lady across the street could help out to make sure that I got to school on time. She promised my mother and father that I could walk with her youngest son, Rob, and his friends.

When I was a kid, Itasca Street seemed longer and busier than Atlanta's Spaghetti Junction. As an adult, however, it seems like everything has shrunken. I point out the houses of some of my childhood friends. Friends I left behind when my mother and father split and we had to move out of the pale-yellow house. We walk around Mattahunt Elementary where I went to grab lunch on hot summer days. I describe our routes for trick-or-treating, where I would come home with pillowcases full of candy. I show the kids the pathway we walked through as a shortcut to school each morning. The once semi-sketchy pathway through the forest is now truly overgrown with trees. How ironic, my shortcut is now for real a scary, dark forest filled with things nightmares are made of.

We end our neighborhood walk back in

front of the light blue house. My connection to this house is so much stronger than the one across the street behind me. My childhood memories are more intact from this house. I only remember bits and pieces of things prior to my escape to safety here.

***

As we head back to the hotel, I am mentally exhausted. I am sad and I've given more of myself today than three or four family tree projects could possibly hold. As I lay my head against the passenger seat, I hear my parents yelling at each other in my head. I see the Subaru being repossessed. I see my father walking out, never to come back and my mother drinking Sprite. Every. Single. Day. I may not remember when we left the pale-yellow house, but I remember that it didn't feel good.

"What was GG-ma like?" asks London as we settle in the hotel room over Chinese takeout. I don't have an appetite, so I've barely touched my food.

"She was a force to be reckoned with, honey. She was strong. She was loving. She loved her family, and she did anything she could to provide for them. GG-ma was the sweetest little lady I've ever known. She would have totally loved you two. You would have watched a lot of Shirley Temple and Country Westerns and it would have been priceless."

"Are you sad that she's in heaven?" Alex asks.

"Sometimes. But I know that she is always watching over us," I say. "I'm going to clear the food; you guys go take a shower and get ready for bed."

As I deal with the feeling of angst beginning to bubble to the surface and overtake my normal and steady composure, I hear James join me. This angst has been sitting right on the edge since Alex first mentioned this trip. The fear, the memories, facing the past, have all been causing anxiety that I've never experienced before. It's like a constant feeling of wanting, no, *needing*, to throw up.

James wraps me in his arms without saying a word. Apparently, I haven't been holding it together as well as I thought I was. At first the tears fall slowly. And then rapidly. Low groans escape my throat as if I am in pain. I *am* in pain, not physically but definitely mentally. The tears continue to fall, despite my attempt to stop them by shutting my eyes tightly, but this time I can't make them stop.

***

I'm not sure what time I fell asleep. Even after I got it together enough to take a shower and get into bed, my sleep was restless. My dreams were vivid and confusing; it was as if my mind was struggling to separate the past from the present. There are glimpses of moments that I don't recall happening and I was on the outside watching the scene unfold. There was a young girl crying over my mother as she laid on the floor passed out. She wasn't responding and the little girl screamed even more. The fear evident in every blood curdling wail. Obviously, the little girl was me, but I can't remember when this event took place or if it's just a figment of my imagination. After jolting awake, I look at my phone and it's 3:14 am. I check on the kids and they are sound asleep, as is James. I lie back down and wait for the Sandman to help me go back to sleep.

***

I hear the kids in the common room in what feel like is only minutes later. I look at my phone and it's a little past eight o'clock. Both kids must have their AirPods in because they are singing two completely different songs. They definitely get

54

their perky morning attitude from their daddy.

I am completely exhausted. My eyes are swollen. My body is sore in every way possible. I feel like I was in a 10-round boxing match and I was not crowned the winner. James is hosting a seminar today, so it is just the kids and me. As much as I want to stay in the bed and not face the outside world until it is time to board the plane, I made my kids a promise.

As I drag myself out of bed, I know I have some decisions to make. Our trip is coming to an end. Alex and London deserve to see Ms. Virginia. But this is going to take some real effort on my part.

I truly have the kindest children who know their mommy very well. I sip my freshly brewed coffee and nibble on a delicious room service breakfast compliments of my children. While letting the coffee work its magic, I gaze out the window and allow myself to get lost in my thoughts.

***

"Renee, we need you to come home." I hear my grandma say over the phone.

I sat in my dorm room, confused—Grandma never called late. I knew something was wrong. I asked about Grandad and Rob. She assured me that everything was okay, but I needed to come home immediately.

Days later, I sat in a funeral home next to Grandma, Granddad, Rob, my father and his new wife, Kim. It all happened so fast. My mother was found dead in her apartment, Grandma was her emergency contact on the rental agreement. There was no life insurance policy, no spouse and a daughter who was just a broke college kid. We did an "economic funeral," which meant a funeral home service and an unmarked grave. There was not much of a repass as I didn't know her family members, so there weren't many guests. Her sons made the journey for her funeral, but we didn't talk much. Promises of "we have to do better about keeping in touch" were made.

After the service, everyone else moved on with their lives and I returned to my mother's apartment to pack it up. There were liquor bottles hidden everywhere. I swear I'd just searched the place a month ago. I found Christmas presents addressed to me, her sons and their kids. Always shopping. She just wasn't there to give them to us. Even at the end, my mother chose Sprite and Bacardi over the children for whom who she'd purchased presents months in advance. I could only imagine that she had to be in tremendous pain to constantly mask it with alcohol. There was a small part of me that felt sorry for her. But the daughter who was neglected due to her addiction grew angrier with every bottle I found.

***

"Mommy, you didn't eat your food," London says as she walks into the room.

"You're right, honey. I wasn't quite hungry. But thank you so much for ordering it for me."

She gives me the biggest, warmest and most comforting hug. It's just what I need. To hold my baby girl in my arms.

"Tell your brother to get dressed," I whisper as I hold London close. I let my sweet daughter go and head to the bathroom. "We're going for a drive."

***

The kids choose to bring Ms. Virginia peace lilies so that she can be at peace and full of strength.

These kids are seriously so thoughtful.

After stopping at the cemetery office and searching for my mother's grave on the lobby computer, the kids and I head to find it. It's still unmarked. It's weird standing here looking at grass. I can't explain my feelings as I look at this place—my mother's final resting place.

Lord Jesus, I hope she is finally resting and at peace.

As I stand here, I want to share some of the good memories of Ms. Virginia with Alex and London. I tell London how her hair was long and thick just like hers. The kids laugh hysterically as I tell them how she used to "do" her hair using brown paper bags. She would wrap her hair tight around ripped up pieces of the bag and wear it around the house like that all day. When she finally unwrapped her hair, her curls will bounce so freely all around her head.

I tell them of her phenomenal ability to bake. When my mother was clean and sober, she was an amazing baker. Cookies, cakes, breads—all from scratch. She would sashay around the kitchen, humming a song, mixing ingredients and creating magic. When she was happy, it showed through her food.

I am also honest and tell them that she had faults and failures, but she never stopped trying. I tell them that I wish we'd had more time together in my adulthood so that I could get to know her.

"Mommy, she sounds complicated," says Alex.

"Yes, she was, baby," I reply.

The car is silent on the way back to the hotel. I think the kids are trying to fully understand Ms. Virginia. Looking at my kids in the rearview mirror, I see the weight of the day on them—not nearly as heavy as it is on me. For the first time in a long time, they don't have their AirPods in their ears. Instead, they are both looking out the window, staring intently at the abyss. I tell my children, "I'm sorry you didn't get to meet Ms. Virginia but at least we all know that she is resting and watching over us."

This has been a heavy day, so I turn on the radio to JAM'N 94.5 and sing along to Michael Jackson's *P.Y.T.* The kids hate when I jam out to "old school music." We pull into the hotel and my annoying singing has helped lighten the mood. The kids have joined forces and become my personal *American Idol* Judges. Apparently, I am not making it past the tryouts. Alex would give Simon Cowell a run for his money.

***

CHAPTER 6

Dinner dates with my father are few and far between, but they aren't forced anymore. My father and stepmom, Kim, still live in Boston and visit us in Atlanta when they can. I actually like Kim a lot; she's different from the other women. It is very clear that my father and Kim are busy being in love and travelling the world, and I'm not mad at that.

Before our trip to Boston comes to an end, we've made plans to have a family dinner with them. As we enter the restaurant, Alex and London run straight into the arms of Grandpa and Nana. James and I are pretty much invisible at the moment. I smile as I watch my father and stepmom dote over our children. While my relationship with my father took a long time to rebuild, I am grateful for time and grace.

Now, my kids are blessed to have a relationship with their Grandpa and Nana. We laugh and enjoy a beautiful lobster dinner. Alex and London's eyes grow large as the whole lobsters are brought to the table. They laugh as their Grandpa and Nana try to understand the latest lingo. Explaining that Tik Tok is not a reference to a clock is probably the highlight of the conversation.

"When are you coming back to visit us in Atlanta? It's been quite a while," I ask my father.

"Well, Kim and I were talking," my father says, "and I think we're going to retire and move down there next year."

The kids can barely contain their excitement at the thought of having their grandparents living closer to them.

As we sip the last of our drinks and the kids collect money from their grandfather, I feel at peace.

I may not have had the dream childhood and relationship with my parents that children deserve, but my children will know and have a great relationship with their grandparents.

I do believe light is starting to break through the forest and it's not so scary after all.

***

"I should have brought some of that lobster sauce home." I hear James mumble as we eat Chinese takeout from our favorite Atlanta spot.

I chuckle.

He's right. I have become accustomed to the Chinese food in Atlanta, but it is definitely not the same as Boston.

As I sip my glass of Moscato, I think of the Boston trip. Surprisingly, the trip to Boston didn't take me out. Yes, it was emotional. Emotional. Emo-tion-al! But through narrating my own story for Alex's project, I got to see a different side of my childhood. I got to see how hard it was, and that against all odds, I survived.

My kids learned a lot about Young Renee and even more about the woman they'd always known as "Ms. Virginia." In sharing my story with them—showing them the street I grew up on and the places where my friends and I used to hang out—I learned a lot about myself in the process.

Yes, the trip opened a bunch of old wounds, but Alex now understands that not every family tree is perfect. There are sometimes offshoots and supports that are added to help the tree stand strong.

Helping Alex with his project has helped me to no longer feel captive to the menacing forest. I feel grateful for the lessons that I am learning from my kids on being resilient and reframing my views. Surprisingly, helping Alex with his family tree has made me want to know more about my own. I found grace for my mother through my children. I found peace on a trip that I feared deep within.

I also think maybe it's time for me to keep my end of the promise between my mother's sons—my brothers—and me.

"Hello?" the man on the phone answers.

"Hello, Allen, long time no hear," I say in the phone. "This is your baby sister."

"Renee?" my mother's son replies.

"Yes, it's me."

***

ACKNOWLEDGEMENTS

First and foremost, I want to say thank you to my Lord and Savior Jesus Christ for placing this story in me to share with the world.

I want to thank my husband who supports all of my ideas and only gives me a side-eye occasionally. You are really my match made in heaven! Thank you for telling me the things that I don't always want to hear and loving me through life and all of its obstacles, heartaches and triumphs.

To my son, Jaden Carter, mommy loves you! This story is proof that God will put something in your spirit and you have to trust Him to get it out. I pray that I always inspire you to go after everything you want because it's already yours.

You are a child of the most high God—don't ever forget that!

To my mommy who is my number one cheerleader; thank you for screaming your love for me from every mountain top! To my stepdad, Lorenzo "Kletus," thank you for being in my corner.

To my mom Carole, thank you for being the best stepmom a girl could ask for.

To the Coby/Earl/Brea family, thank you for raising a man who loves me and treasures our family. Thank you for making me a part of your family from day one.

To my sisters – Amanda, Kerrie, Jonelle, Syeeta – Your excitement about this book is what motivated me to complete it. Thank you for your encouragement every time the forest was too overwhelming. Your love and support through this process has meant everything.

Mandy!!!!!!! I don't even know where to start or how to put into words how appreciative I am of you! You just don't know what a bright light you are in my life and in this book. This story has been in my spirit for so long. THANK YOU for helping me to birth it and make it a reality. Thank you for all the editing, suggestions and pushing me to be a "real" writer. A. Lee Hughes is a real author y'all—please read her books! They will bless your life. Shout out to my tribe of amazing women who love me in my craziest form—"I belong to this tribe."

To my mother, sisters, brother, sister-cousins, brother-cousins, nieces, nephews, aunts, uncles, cousins and everyone else who I wouldn't want to dear forget—thank you for contributing to this adventure called life and for loving me in your own special way.

And finally, thank you to you, the reader. I hope that you enjoyed Renee's adventure and my creative freedom as much as I enjoyed creating it for you.

ABOUT THE AUTHOR

Maria Anderson was born and raised in Boston, Massachusetts. Her faith is her foundation and her family is her motivation. She is a foodie who loves trying new restaurants, food trucks or anywhere with a good taco! Maria loves to travel, especially to warmer climates that have drinks with umbrellas, and she loves spending time with friends and family making memories and living life to the fullest. Maria also owns an event planning business, Center of Attention, where she celebrates life's most precious moments and makes her clients the center of attention on their special day.

Maria currently lives in Florida with her husband and son. *The Other Side of Fear* is her debut novelette.

Made in the USA
Columbia, SC
12 March 2021